"Here we are!" Ben stopped at a pen and beckoned Laura over to the wire.

At first Laura thought the pen was empty. But when she bent down, she could see a tiny dog, no bigger than a kitten, cowering in a corner at the back. It was covered in patchy white fur that reminded her of the downy baby bird.

"Oh!" Laura gasped, feeling her heart go out to it.

The puppy looked up at her with the saddest, most beautiful almond-shaped eyes she had ever seen.

"Hello, little dog," Laura said softly.

The puppy tilted its head to one side, and gazed longingly into her eyes . . .

"Laura, I"d like you and your family to meet someone special," Ben said. "His name is Bertie . . ."

Have you read all these books in the **Battersea Dogs & Cats Home** series?

BERTIE'S
story

by

Jane Clarke

Illustrated by Sharon Rentta
Puzzle illustrations by Jason Chapman

RED FOX

BATTERSEA DOGS AND CATS HOME: BERTIE'S STORY
A RED FOX BOOK 978 1 849 41581 1

First published in Great Britain by Red Fox,
an imprint of Random House Children's Books
A Random House Group Company

This edition published 2012

1 3 5 7 9 10 8 6 4 2

The Random House Group Limited supports the Forest Stewardship Council
(FSC®), the leading international forest certification organization. Our books
carrying the FSC label are printed on FSC®-certified paper. FSC is the only
forest certification scheme endorsed by the leading environmental
organizations, including Greenpeace. Our paper procurement policy can be
found at www.randomhouse.co.uk/environment.

MIX
Paper from
responsible sources
FSC® C016897

Set in 13/20 Stone Informal

Red Fox Books are published by Random House Children's Books,
61–63 Uxbridge Road, London W5 5SA

www.**kids**at**randomhouse**.co.uk
www.**totallyrandombooks**.co.uk

Addresses for companies within The Random House Group Limited
can be found at: www.randomhouse.co.uk/offices.htm

THE RANDOM HOUSE GROUP Limited Reg. No. 954009

A CIP catalogue record for this book is available from the British Library.

Printed and bound in Great Britain by
CPI Bookmarque, Croydon, CR0 4TD

Turn to page 89 for lots
of information on
Battersea Dogs & Cats Home,
plus some cool activities!

🐾 🐾 🐾 🐾

Meet the stars of the Battersea Dogs & Cats Home series to date . . .

Bailey

Chester

Misty

Max

Rusty

Daisy

Snowy

Huey

Stella

Angel

Cosmo

Alfie

Buddy and Holly

Coco

Petal

Suzy

Bertie

Laura to the Rescue!

Eight-year-old Laura Downing was sitting in the garden daydreaming, when something landed with a *thump!* on the grass beside her.

It was a tiny baby bird. It lay on its back, not moving.

"Dad!" she yelled. "Come quick!"

She bent over the tiny creature. It had a bright yellow beak that looked much

too big for its pink downy body. The
speckled feathers on its wings were ruffled
and its eyes were tightly shut.

"Poor little thing!" she murmured.

Her dad put down the gardening fork
he had been weeding with, and knelt
down beside her.

"It must have fallen out of its nest," he
said softly. "Is it still breathing?"

"I . . . I think so," Laura
whispered. "Yes, I can
see its chest rising
and falling!" She
sighed with
relief.

Dad peered into the apple tree.

"It's had quite a fall," he said. "The nest is near the top of the tree. I can try to put it back, but I think it needs a quiet safe place to recover first."

"I know where there's a box!" Laura ran into the house and dashed into her teenage sister's room. Leah was lying on the bed, listening to music.

"I need to borrow that shoebox your new trainers are in!" Laura rummaged in the bottom of Leah's wardrobe.

"Hey!" Leah yelled as Laura tipped out her sister's shoes, raced off to the bathroom, grabbed a hand towel and rushed back out to the garden.

"That will do nicely," Dad commented as Laura carefully lined the shoebox with the towel.

She scooped up the baby bird and gently laid it inside the box. The chick's eyes fluttered and opened.

"Hello, birdy," Laura whispered. "Don't be scared, I'll keep you safe."

There was a clatter as Leah threw open the door to the garden. She stood in the doorway with one hand on her hip and the other pointing to the

shoebox. Laura put her finger to her lips.

"It was an emergency!" she told her big sister. "This little bird fell out of its nest!"

"That was stupid of it!" Leah declared as she slouched over and peered into the box.

"Its mum and dad probably pushed it out to encourage it to fly," Dad explained. "The poor thing clearly wasn't quite ready."

"How unfair!" Laura gasped. "It's like you and Mum pushing me out onto the street when I was a baby to make me walk!"

"Sometimes I wish they had!" Leah muttered.

There was a tiny *cheep!* from the box.
Laura watched as the
baby bird rolled
onto its tummy
and opened its
beak. Its
feathers were
patchy and
scruffy-looking
with tufts of
down sticking
up between
them.

"Dad's right
about you not being
ready to fly," Laura commented. "Your
feathers are still growing . . ."

Leah peered at the little bird and
shuddered.

"It's *soooo* ugly," she remarked.

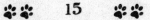

"Maybe it's hungry! I'll find some worms!" Laura picked up her dad's gardening fork and hurried towards the flowerbed. She could hear Leah making *yuk* noises as she turned over the crumbly earth and picked out a soft, juicy worm.

Laura carefully dangled the worm over the fledgling's beak. To her delight, it gobbled it down like a string of fat spaghetti, and cheeped again.

"You must be thirsty, I'll get you some water," she told the little bird in a soft voice. "Then I'll make some holes in the box lid, cover you up and leave you to recover in peace."

"You're looking after it really well," Dad told Laura. "I'm sure this little bird will soon be ready to be returned to the nest."

"Great. Then I can have my box back!" Leah stomped back to her bedroom.

"It's good practice for being a vet when I grow up," Laura smiled wistfully. "I wish I could have a pet I could care for all the time!"

A Big Surprise

The next morning, as soon as it was
light, Laura leaped out of bed and
hurtled downstairs. She'd left the shoebox
in a quiet corner of the kitchen overnight.
Laura held her breath as she opened the
lid. But there was no need to worry. The
fledgling's eyes were bright and sparkling
and it was cheeping hungrily!

Laura dashed back upstairs.

"The baby bird's fine!" she announced happily. "It's ready to go back to the nest!"

There was a groan from Leah's bedroom. "Stop making all that noise!" she moaned. "It's much too early to get up!"

"I'll fetch the ladder!" Dad said, with a yawn. He made his way into the garden, still wearing his pyjamas, closely followed by Mum in her dressing gown. Mum held onto the bottom of the ladder while Dad tucked the box under one arm, climbed the ladder and carefully placed the tiny bird back in its nest. Laura hopped excitedly from foot to foot.

"Will it be OK?" she asked as her dad put the ladder away.

"I'm sure it will be," he reassured her. "The mum's hopping around in the tree collecting insects to feed it with. Now, how about we go in for *our* breakfast?"

"Good idea, I'll put the kettle on." Mum headed for the kitchen.

Leah was sitting at the breakfast table, hunched over a mug of coffee, scowling.

"Here's your box back," Laura told Leah. "The baby bird's OK! Its mum and dad will look after it until its feathers have grown properly and it can fly."

Leah raised an eyebrow. "I don't know why you're so bothered about some scrawny little bird," she told Laura. "It's the runt of the nest – like you!"

Laura's face fell. She hated it when Leah reminded her how small she was.

"Don't be so mean!" Dad told Leah. "Laura's a lovely, sensitive soul who always wants to help any creature in trouble."

"Too sensitive if you ask me!" Leah snorted. "Remember how upset she got when I caught that enormous spider in my bedroom? I was going to  flush it down the toilet, but Laura made such a fuss. She begged Mum to stop me and I had to take the horrid thing outside instead."

Laura could feel tears welling up in her eyes as her big sister made fun of her.

"Cheer up!" Mum said, giving her a big hug and glaring at Leah. "We love the way you care for things, Laura." Mum glanced at Dad and he nodded. "In fact, we've been talking a lot lately about how we think you might be ready to care for a pet . . ."

Laura jumped to her feet. "What sort of pet?" she gasped.

There was a huge smile on Dad's face. "How would you like to go to Battersea Dogs & Cats Home to choose a puppy to look after?" he asked. "We've been

checking it out, and we can make an
appointment to see them next Saturday!"

"Yes, yes! Yes!" Laura squealed in
delight. "I love dogs! I've read stories
about Battersea! They're amazing. They
aim to never turn away a dog or cat in
need of a home . . ."

Leah's mouth dropped open. "I've

been asking for a cute
little Chihuahua for
AGES!" she
moaned. "How
come you say
yes to Laura
and not to me?"
"The new
puppy will be
part of the
family, for
everyone to share,"

Dad explained. "We love you very much, Leah, but right now, we're not sure you would look after a dog properly. Laura has proved she can care for things and we know she'll spend a lot of time and energy looking after it."

Laura felt as if she'd burst with pride and happiness. They were going to have a puppy from Battersea! What could be better than giving a dog a new home? She was over the moon!

The Right Choice

The week seemed to go on forever, but at last Saturday arrived and Laura was sitting next to Leah in the back of the car. They were on their way to Battersea Dogs & Cats Home!

Laura's tummy felt as if it was full of butterflies and her heart was thumping with excitement. It was the most important day of her life! They were

going to choose a dog to
care for for ever and
ever! She could hardly
bear to wait a
moment longer.

"Keep still!" Leah
groaned, not taking her
eyes off her mobile phone.
"I can't text with you wriggling about."

But there was no way Laura could
keep still. The instant Dad found a
parking space and unlocked the back
doors, she leaped out of
the car.

"Hurry up!" she
begged as Leah
yawned, slowly
flipped her phone
shut and clambered
out of the car.

Laura raced up to the front gate. She was so excited she could hardly speak. "We've come to re-dog a home!" she told the man.

Leah rolled her eyes.

The man smiled at Laura. "You need Dog Reception – just past our new

cattery," he told her.

Laura gazed in awe at the circular glass building. Cats of all shapes and sizes were looking down at them from every window. She nudged Leah and pointed them out.

"Cool," Leah said grudgingly.

A friendly-looking man greeted them
at the Reception desk.

"You must be the Downing family," he
said. "My name's Ben. Before I take you
to meet our dogs, I'll ask you a few
questions to help you choose
a good match for your
family . . ."

"Like how big our house and garden is,
and what size of dog we want, and how
much time we can spend walking it and

playing with it . . ." Laura rattled through the questions. "I've read all about the interview. It's very important. And so is the home visit before we collect our new pet . . ."

"It is," Ben smiled.

"Mum will look after it during the day," Laura announced. "I'll be in charge first thing in the morning, after school and at weekends! And I promise I will always and forever take brilliant care of him, whoever he – or she – may be!"

"Laura's a very caring person," Mum added. "She wants to be a vet when she grows up."

Laura nodded. "I've already looked after a baby bird and returned it to its nest!" she told Ben.

"Well done," Ben said. He asked more questions and filled in their answers on the application form. Then he put down the pen, and looked at them thoughtfully. Laura looked eagerly back at him. Ben smiled.

"There's one special little dog I'd particularly like Laura to meet," he said. "Follow me!" And he led them to the dog pens.

There were so many
dogs needing a new
home! It was hard for
Laura to walk past
them without stopping
to say hello. A gorgeous,
glossy Doberman
tipped his head on one side
as he spotted her, and a
very friendly Staffordshire
Bull Terrier jumped up
with her front paws on
the wire, wagging
her tail. A yellow
Labrador with big
chocolate-coloured eyes
pressed his nose to the wire
and snuffled at them. His
ears fell slightly as the
Downing family walked by.

"Your dogs are all *brilliant!*" Laura declared as they hurried after Ben. She'd be happy to take any of them home – or all of them, if only she could!

"Have you got any cute little Chihuahuas that would fit in my handbag?" Leah asked Ben.

"We haven't," Ben replied gently. "To be honest, we think it's wrong for pets to be carried around in handbags like fashion accessories."

"Oh!" Leah went pink and looked a bit ashamed.

"Here we are!" Ben stopped at a pen and beckoned Laura over to the wire.

At first Laura thought the pen was empty. But when she bent down, she could see a tiny dog, no bigger than a kitten, cowering in a corner at the back. It was covered in patchy white fur that reminded her of the downy baby bird.

"Oh!" Laura gasped, feeling her heart go out to it.

The puppy looked up at her with the saddest, most beautiful almond-shaped eyes she had ever seen.

"Hello, little dog," Laura said softly.

The puppy tilted its head to one side, and gazed longingly into her eyes . . .

"Laura, I'd like you and your family to meet someone special," Ben said. "His name is Bertie . . ."

Bertie's Lucky Day

"Bertie's a West Highland Terrier," Ben explained. "He has a very sweet nature, but as you can see, he can be nervous. He's lost most of his hair because he was totally neglected by his previous owner. Someone left him outside the Home in the middle of the night! We found him the next morning tied to the front gates with a bit of old rope. Bertie was in a pitiful state, stick-thin and shaking all over because he was so frightened."

"You poor little thing!" Laura murmured.

At the sound of her voice, Bertie's tail gave a tiny wag.

Ben opened the door and beckoned Laura into the pen. She crouched down, being careful not to make any sudden movements that might scare Bertie. The little Westie sniffed at her outstretched hand and gazed at her with his sad eyes. Laura held her breath as he pattered slowly up to her. Now he was closer, she could see the puppy's pink skin

beneath his fuzzy tufts of fur. She gently
stroked his cute fluffy ears. They were the
only part of him where the hair was
growing properly.

"Awww!" she breathed. She
glanced at her family. Leah
was scowling, but Mum
and Dad were
smiling, and so
was Ben.

"Bertie's weight is almost back to what it should be," Ben went on, "but his coat is taking a very long time to grow back and he hasn't got much confidence. What he needs is a loving home, good food and lots of attention and walks in the fresh air."

"He looks like that scrawny baby bird that fell out of its nest!" Leah said sniffily. "I'd *much* rather have that lovely yellow Labrador we passed before."

"That's the sort of thing everyone says when they come to pick a dog," Ben sighed. "And that's why poor little Bertie is still living here. On average, it takes our dogs around forty-eight days to be re-homed, but Bertie's been here for over three months. He's becoming one of our longest-serving residents!"

Laura turned to her mum and dad. Her eyes were shining.

"Please let's choose Bertie," she begged. "He's so in need of a new home! I'll really, really love him and look after him and make him better . . ."

Mum and Dad looked at each other.

"With the right care, Bertie will grow up to be a lovely dog," Ben reassured them.

Laura crossed her fingers behind her back and held her breath. What if her family sided with Leah?

Mum nodded slowly.

"If anyone can fix Bertie, it's our Laura," Dad said proudly.

"Bertie! It's your lucky day!" Ben told the little Westie. "It looks like you've found a new home!"

Bertie's stumpy tail began to wag.

"It's my lucky day, too!" Laura declared, wiping a tear of joy from her eyes.

A Wobbly Start

At long last, it was dog day! Laura grabbed her school bag and raced out of the classroom the instant the bell went.

After their visit to Battersea, Dad had dog-proofed the garden by putting a wire fence up and Mum and Laura had fun buying all the things that Bertie would need. Then someone from the Home had visited to check that their house was suitable. It was! Laura had never been so excited!

"Can't stop," Laura told her school friends. "Mum and Dad are picking up our new puppy this afternoon – they could be home already!"

Laura dashed to the house. She was just in time. The car was pulling into the drive. Mum got out of the back seat, cradling Bertie in her arms. He was shaking from nose to tail.

"He was scared in the car," Mum whispered as she carried the little Westie into the house and set him down in his basket in the hallway. "It must be very confusing for him."

"Don't worry, Bertie, you're home now," Laura said soothingly. She knelt down beside her puppy and gently stroked him behind his ears. Bertie gradually stopped shaking and looked up trustingly at her. Then he rolled over and let her tickle his pink tummy. His stubby tail wagged.

"Come and see where you live." Laura clipped Bertie's lead onto his collar and gently encouraged him out of the basket. Mum and Dad followed as she proudly led Bertie from room to room, letting him sniff curiously at everything.

Suddenly the front door crashed open. Bertie jumped like he'd been stung by a bee and dashed behind Laura's legs. She could feel him shaking.

"I'm back!" Leah shouted. "Where is he?" Her footsteps echoed up the hall.

Bertie crouched down and made a puddle on the living room carpet.

"You nearly scared him to death!" Laura said as Leah entered the room. "You know Bertie is a nervous dog after all he's been through."

"So-*rry*!" Leah said sarcastically, "I didn't know he'd wet himself, did I?"

"Laura, why don't you and Leah take Bertie for a walk and show him the park?" Mum said in her this-is-an-order-not-a-question voice.

"But I've got to call Jake," Leah replied.

"You've spent all day at school with Jake," Mum said firmly. "It's important that you get to know Bertie and Bertie gets to know you."

"If I must!" Leah moaned. But once they'd left the house, she mooched along beside Laura and Bertie, texting on her mobile and not paying them any attention. Laura didn't care. She was having a lovely time – and so was Bertie. The little Westie seemed much more confident outside. He was trotting along perkily, snuffling at all the lampposts and trees along the road.

"We're going to have such fun now you've come to live with us!" Laura told Bertie gleefully as they went through the park gates. "You'll love the park. There are lots of squirrels!"

Bertie's ears pricked up and his tail wagged as Laura headed for the path running through the centre of the park.

"No! This way!" Leah grabbed Laura by the arm and dragged her and Bertie down a side path.

"What's up?" Laura asked, puzzled.

Leah pointed to a group of teenagers on the main path. "I don't want my mates from school to see me with my kid sister and her ugly dog!" she hissed.

"Ugly?" Laura bent
down and covered
Bertie's ears. "He's
not ugly!" she
exclaimed.
"That's a really
mean thing to
say!"

"It's true,"
Leah pouted. "You
chose the ugliest
dog in Battersea!"

"Well, he won't be ugly forever, but
you will *always* be mean!" Laura retorted.
They were so busy arguing they didn't
notice that Leah's friends had spotted
them and were coming their way.

"Hey, Leah!" one of the boys shouted.
It was Jake. "What have you got there? A
big bald rat?"

Yip! Bertie woofed, and tried to run away, but Laura was holding him on the lead, so all he could do was skitter round in circles.

"Look at it chasing its ratty tail!" Jake went on. The group of teenagers sniggered.

"Call that a dog?"

"Hey, Jake, give me a break! It's my kid sister's!" Leah told him. "Little Laura chose it because she thinks she can make it better."

"She'll need magic to turn that scrawny rat into a proper dog!" Jake laughed, and all the teenagers joined in, including Leah.

Bertie's tail drooped and he began to quiver. A puddle appeared on the ground between his back legs.

"It's not just any old rat, it's a water rat!" Jake commented. They all fell around laughing.

"You're the rats, not him!" Laura muttered under her breath. She scooped up Bertie and turned away before they could see her cry. Bertie had been having such fun, and now he was shaking from nose to tail. How could Leah and her friends be so cruel? Laura couldn't bear it. Tears poured down her face and dripped off the end of her nose onto Bertie's patchy coat.

Caring for Each Other

Laura sank down behind a leafy bush, out of sight from Leah and her friends. "It's not fair to treat you like that after everything you've been through!" Laura sobbed as she cuddled her poor little puppy. In the safety of her arms, Bertie soon stopped shaking. He gently licked the end of Laura's nose with his soft pink tongue until she stopped crying. Laura couldn't help smiling. Bertie seemed to know how upset she was, and was trying to comfort her!

Laura wiped away her tears and glanced between the leaves. There was no sign of Leah and her friends. They must have gone off somewhere. Laura sighed with relief as she gently set Bertie down on the ground.

Bertie cocked his head to one side and gave a little *woof*.

Laura threw her arms around him. "It doesn't matter what Leah and her horrible friends think," she told her little Westie. "To me, you're the very best dog in the whole wide world! And I'm going to take you home and look after you for ever and ever. The only magic you need is love!"

Bertie's tail wagged as Laura led him home and opened the front door.

She poked her head into
the living room. Mum
had cleared up the
puddle. Laura could
hear her clattering
around in the
kitchen.

"We're back!"
Laura called. "Leah's
stayed in the park
with her friends."

Mum appeared at
the kitchen door. "How
did you and Bertie get on?" she asked.

"OK – until Leah's friends made fun of
him." Laura sighed. "I've decided the best
thing to do is ignore them!"

"Good plan!" Mum agreed. "I must get
on with the cooking. Bring Bertie into the
kitchen when he's ready for his dinner."

"He needs grooming first." Laura reached up to the shelf above Bertie's bed and took the soft dog brush that Battersea had recommended for Bertie's poor coat. He stood patiently as she slowly and carefully brushed him from nose to tail. After a minute or two, Laura felt him relax. He gave a deep sigh of contentment and rolled over so that Laura could gently brush the tufts of fur on his tummy. His eyes closed. They opened again the moment she stopped brushing.

"Dinner time now," Laura told him, and she led him into the kitchen. Mum helped her open a tin of smelly dog food and watched as she put a couple of spoonfuls into Bertie's new bowl.

"You're taking such good care of him!" Mum commented.

Bertie's almond-shaped eyes sparkled as Laura put his food down in font of him. He ate up every bit and wagged his tail for more!

Dad came in from the garden.

"Good to see Bertie's doing better!" he exclaimed.

Woof! Bertie trotted into the hall and fetched the ball Laura had put in his basket. He dropped it at her feet. *Woof!* he repeated.

"He wants to play!" Dad said. "That's fantastic progress!"

Laura grinned from ear to ear as she picked up the ball and let Bertie out into the garden.

As she stepped onto the grass, there was a rustle in the leaves of the apple tree above them. A cute little sparrow was fluttering from branch to branch. It settled on the nest and chirped down at her. It had to be the baby bird!

Laura's heart filled with joy as she tossed the ball and Bertie scampered after it. She wouldn't let herself care what Leah and her friends thought. The baby bird had turned out fine, and so would Bertie. And better still, Bertie was having fun – and so was she!

Things Look Up

"Bertie's looking bright-eyed and bushy-tailed this morning!" Dad remarked, laying down the Sunday papers on the breakfast table so he could watch the little puppy trot round the kitchen with his rubber bone toy in his mouth.

"He looks very happy," Mum agreed. "And his fur has grown back a lot in the two weeks he's been with us! He's a credit to you, Laura."

Laura beamed.

"He's got a long way to go before I'd be caught dead with him out in public!" Leah muttered. "He still looks more like a rat than a dog to me!"

At the sound of Leah's grumpy voice, Bertie took his toy bone and lay down in his favourite safe place – between Laura's feet.

"Leah! If you insist on being mean, you can leave the room," Mum said with a frown.

"No problem! I'm going to light some scented candles and have a nice long luxurious bath." Leah flounced off. She paused at the door and pointed at Laura and Bertie. "I do NOT want to be interrupted," she said.

Mum and Dad looked at each other. "Typical teenager!" they mouthed.

Laura giggled. She picked up her new book about dogs and headed out into the garden. Bertie trotted after her and settled contentedly beside her in the shade of the apple tree. Laura shaded her eyes against the hot sunshine and gazed into the tree, but the sparrows' nest seemed to be empty.

She was just thinking
that they must have all flown away when
Leah threw open the bathroom window.
She stuck out her tongue at Laura and
Bertie, then pulled the curtains closed,
leaving them flapping in the breeze.

Laura ignored her and turned to her book. She was reading about how to teach dogs tricks when, all of a sudden, Bertie leaped to his feet and rushed into the house.

Laura threw the book down on the grass and raced after him. Bertie was bounding up the stairs. Laura could hear the sound of water running into the bath, and loud music thumping out of Leah's room.

"Come down!" Laura ordered Bertie. "Leah will be angry if you disturb her!"

But it was no good. Bertie stood on the landing and began to bark.

"Shhh!" Laura hissed, dashing up the stairs.

The instant she got to the top, Bertie began to jump up and down on all fours.

Woof! woof! woof! he barked. He dashed round in a circle and nosed at the bathroom door.

"What are you trying to tell me?"
Laura asked, puzzled. But before she
could work out what it was, Leah came
charging out of her room, her face
covered in bright pink face mask.

"Get that ratty puppy out of here!" she
screeched, "or you'll both be sorry!"

Brave Bertie

Woof! Bertie pushed past Leah and hurled himself at the bathroom door. It swung open and a cloud of steam billowed out, and something else – smoke!

Leah's mouth dropped open, making cracks in the pink face mask.

Laura peered round the door.

The bottom of one of the curtains was smouldering. The breeze had blown it onto a candle that Leah had lit on the windowsill!

"Fire!" Laura yelled.

Woof! woof! woof!

Bertie barked.

Mum and Dad bounded up the stairs.
Dad took one look and ripped the curtain
off the curtain rail. He dumped it in the

bath. Mum grabbed the toilet brush and pushed the curtain under water before it could burst into flames.

"Leah! We've told you never, ever to light a candle anywhere near the curtains!" Mum said sternly.

"You could have burned the house down and everything in it – including yourself!" Dad exclaimed with a frown.

Leah clapped her hands over her mouth.

"I . . . I . . . I'm sorry! I didn't think!" she said shakily, forgetting to use her grumpy teenage voice.

"It's a good job Bertie noticed it when he did!" Laura told her.

"It really, really is!" Leah replied thoughtfully, looking at the burned curtain floating in the bath. "If Bertie hadn't noticed, it could have been a whole lot worse!" she said in a small voice.

To Laura's amazement, Leah stroked
Bertie on the back.

"Good boy! That was a very clever
thing to do," Leah told him. "Jake
shouldn't have called you a rat!"

Laura's mouth dropped open. Bertie stared in surprise at Leah's pink face, and his tail twitched uncertainly.

"He's a real hero!" Laura added. "He stuck around even when you were shouting at him!"

Leah turned to Laura. "That was brave!" she admitted. Leah took a deep breath and looked at her toes. "I'm sorry I've been so nasty to Bertie – I'll try to be nicer to him, and to you in the future. Jake's wrong. Bertie's not ratty, he's a sweet puppy, really."

Leah bent down
and gently
stroked Bertie
behind the
ears. Bertie
wagged his
tail.

"It looks
like Bertie
accepts your
apology,"
Laura said
solemnly, "and
so do I!"

Dad smiled.
"That's what we like
to hear!" he remarked.

"Take Bertie downstairs," Mum told
Laura. "Leah's going to help clean up the
mess, aren't you?" Leah nodded.

Bertie bounced down the stairs after Laura. She led him into the kitchen and reached for the box of doggy biscuits.

"You deserve a treat!" she told him.

Bertie gave a little woof, then wagged his tail as he crunched up his bone-shaped cookie.

"You're the funniest, cleverest, bravest puppy ever!" Laura said, throwing her arms around him.

She couldn't help noticing that the little Westie felt soft and cuddly and

much furrier than when she'd first met
him. But that wasn't the most important
thing. What really, really mattered was
that Mum and Dad and even Leah were
all glad she'd chosen to bring him home!

"Bertie, you're the best!" Laura
beamed. "Everyone knows that now!"

Read on for lots more . . .

🐾 🐾 🐾 🐾

Battersea Dogs & Cats Home

Battersea Dogs & Cats Home is a charity that aims never to turn away a dog or cat in need of our help. We reunite lost dogs and cats with their owners; when we can't do this, we care for them until new homes can be found for them; and we educate the public about responsible pet ownership. Every year the Home takes in around 10,000 dogs and cats. In addition to the site in southwest London, the Home also has two other centres based at Old Windsor, Berkshire, and Brands Hatch, Kent.

The original site in Holloway

History

The Temporary Home for Lost and Starving Dogs was originally opened in a stable yard in Holloway in 1860 by Mary Tealby after she found a starving puppy in the street. There was no one to look after him, so she took him home and nursed him back to health. She was so worried about the other dogs wandering the streets that she opened the Temporary Home for Lost and Starving Dogs. The Home was established to help to look after them all and find them new owners.

Sadly Mary Tealby died in 1865, aged sixty-four, and little more is known about her, but her good work was continued. In 1871 the Home moved to its present site in Battersea, and was renamed the Dogs' Home Battersea.

Some important dates for the Home:

1883 – Battersea start taking in cats.

1914 – 100 sledge dogs are housed at the Hackbridge site, in preparation for Ernest Shackleton's second Antarctic expedition.

1956 – Queen Elizabeth II becomes patron of the Home.

2004 – Red the Lurcher's night-time antics become world famous when he is caught on camera regularly escaping from his kennel and liberating his canine chums for midnight feasts.

2007 – The BBC broadcast *Animal Rescue Live* from the Home for three weeks from mid-July to early August.

Amy Watson

Amy Watson has been working at
Battersea Dogs & Cats Home for eight
years and has been the Home's Education
Officer for four years. Amy's role means
that she organizes all the school visits to
the Home for children aged sixteen and
under, and regularly visits schools around
Battersea's three sites to teach children

how to behave and stay safe around dogs and cats, and all about responsible dog and cat ownership. She also regularly features on the Battersea website – www.battersea.org.uk – giving tips and advice on how to train your dog or cat under the "Fun and Learning" section.

On most school visits Amy can take a dog with her, so she is normally accompanied by her beautiful ex-Battersea dog, Hattie. Hattie has been living with Amy for three years and really enjoys meeting new children and helping Amy with her work.

The process for re-homing a dog or a cat

When a lost dog or cat arrives, Battersea's Lost Dogs & Cats Line works hard to try to find the animal's owners. If, after seven days, they have not been able to reunite them, the search for a new home can begin.

The Home works hard to find caring, permanent new homes for all the lost and unwanted dogs and cats.

Dogs and cats have their own characters and so staff at the Home will spend time getting to know every dog and cat. This helps decide the type of home the dog or cat needs.

There are three stages of the re-homing process at Battersea Dogs & Cats Home. Battersea's re-homing team wants to find you the perfect pet: sometimes this can take a while, so please be patient while we search for your new friend!

1 Register details

2 Match

3 Leaving with your new pet

Have a look at our website:
http://www.battersea.org.uk/dogs/rehoming/index.html for more details!

"Did you know?" questions about dogs and cats

- Puppies do not open their eyes until they are about two weeks old.

- According to *Guinness World Records*, the smallest living dog is a long-haired Chihuahua called Danka Kordak from Slovakia, who is 13.8cm tall and 18.8cm long.

- Dalmatians, with all those cute black spots, are actually born white.

- The greyhound is the fastest dog on earth. It can reach speeds of up to 45 miles per hour.

- The first living creature sent into space was a female dog named Laika.

- Cats spend 15% of their day grooming themselves and a massive 70% of their day sleeping.

- Cats see six times better in the dark than we do.

- A cat's tail helps it to balance when it is on the move – especially when it is jumping.

- The cat, giraffe and camel are the only animals that walk by moving both their left feet, then both their right feet, when walking.

Dos and Don'ts of looking after dogs and cats

Dogs dos and don'ts

DO

- Be gentle and quiet around dogs at all times – treat them how you would like to be treated.
- Have respect for dogs.

DON'T

- Sneak up on a dog – you could scare them.
- Tease a dog – it's not fair.
- Stare at a dog – dogs can find this scary.
- Disturb a dog who is sleeping or eating.

- Assume a dog wants to play with you. Just like you, sometimes they may want to be left alone.
- Approach a dog who is without an owner as you won't know if the dog is friendly or not.

Cats dos and don'ts

DO
- Be gentle and quiet around cats at all times.
- Have respect for cats.
- Let a cat approach you in their own time.

DON'T
- Never stare at a cat as they can find this intimidating.

- Tease a cat – it's not fair.
- Disturb a sleeping or eating cat – they may not want attention or to play.
- Assume a cat will always want to play. Like you, sometimes they want to be left alone.

Some fun pet-themed puzzles!

What to think about before getting a dog!

Here is a list of things that you need to think about before getting a dog. See if you can find them in the word search and while you look, think why they might be so important. Only look for words written in black. They can be written backwards, diagonally, forwards, up and down, so look carefully and GOOD LUCK!

```
I N D E P E N D E N T U N O P M S D H W
S X C V B N H R D G H I L J A N E V X Q
S F T I M E A L O N E N M K E R Q U S P
G T H S W V B J P X Z D F E H I Y J T M
A C V B O M G D F D S C T Y A A O P R W
F R O U Z C H I L D R E N C Y L I O A K
G D V B I D F J L Q W E V Z L C O Z N R
T G H Y J K L H M N F D S E R T Y J K E M
M U I L D F G O H K V M F E T Y J K E M O
A G H D N C V U B C V P O G M T R I R O
L W X D Z V G S I Z E B F C E X P Z S I
E T Q U A D B E H D L N K Y A G E J G L
O R J C O A T T Y P E N B C X S T F H J
F O R X A O K A Q E N S N M Y I E Q Z L
E N E R G E T I C P A S V F H B N H X K
M W D F B V H N L K G R U O I V A H E B
A S Q E T R Y I D A C X B U K O Y T F C
L Q D S T R O N G W I L L E D N J M X Z
E H I G V N H K G N I N I A R T C I S A B
```

- SIZE
- MALE OR FEMALE
- AGE
- COAT TYPE
- COST
- BEHAVIOUR
- BASIC TRAINING
- HOUSE TRAINING
- TIME ALONE
- GOOD WITH: PETS, CHILDREN, STRANGERS, DOGS
- HOW: ENERGETIC, CUDDLY, STRONG WILLED, INDEPENDENT

Can you think of any other things? Write them in the spaces below.

Remember: when training a dog, reward works better than punishment.

Tangled Leads and Crazy Maze

Oh dear! The Battersea staff are walking three dogs but the leads are tangled. Can you find out which dog belongs to which person by following the leads?

Chris

Michelle

George

Spikey

Joe

Sammy

Tessa

Start here

Who's walking who?
George is walking ------
Michelle is walking ------
Chris is walking ------

Remember: while in public all dogs must wear a collar and tag and should be kept on a lead.

Remember: always take a poop-scoop bag with you and clean up after your dog.

"Yummy yummy. Three big juicy bones for me," says Tessa, but can you help her find her way through the maze to find the bones?

Drawing dogs and cats

If you can draw these shapes you can draw a dog:

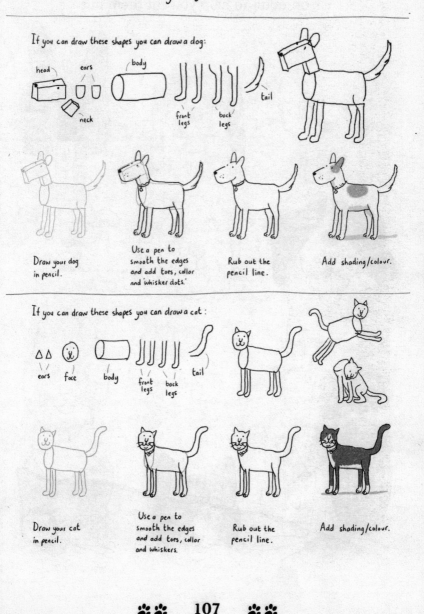

head   ears   body   tail

neck   front   back
legs   legs

Draw your dog in pencil.

Use a pen to smooth the edges and add toes, collar and 'whisker dots.'

Rub out the pencil line.

Add shading/colour.

If you can draw these shapes you can draw a cat :

ears   face   body   tail

front   back
legs   legs

Draw your cat in pencil.

Use a pen to smooth the edges and add toes, collar and whiskers.

Rub out the pencil line.

Add shading/colour.

Making a Mask

Copy these faces onto a piece of paper and
ask an adult to help you cut them out.

Dog Breeds Crossword

Across

2 A breed used as police dogs and sometimes called an Alsatian. (6,8)

5 A dog that is a mixture of breeds. (7)

6 A breed commonly used as guide dogs for the blind. (8)

9 Smallest breed of dog. (9)

11 A brown/liver and white breed often referred to as sniffer dogs. (8,7)

14 A French breed with very curly hair, traditionally used as a gun dog. (6)

15 A small black and tan terrier that was used to catch rats. (6)

16 A small white terrier from Scotland. (6)

17 A small breed with short legs and a long back, sometimes called a sausage dog. (9)

18 The dog often used as the symbol of Great Britain. (7)

Down

2 A spotted dog from a Disney film that needs lots of walking as a pet. (9)

3 A breed associated with a brand of paint. (3,7,8)

4 This breed is used to herd sheep and needs lots of activity such as agility if kept as a pet. (6,6)

7 Eddie from the programme *Frasier* is one of these. (11)

8 A breed associated with a brand of shoes. (6,5)

10 Scooby Doo was one of these very large dogs. (9)

12 These dogs are used for racing but also make good pets. (9)

13 Smaller version of 'Lassie' dog. (7)

Help!
All is trying to count the dogs but some of them keep running about.
How many can you count?

Remember: all dogs need exercise in order to keep them fit and healthy and to give mental stimulation.

109

Here is a delicious recipe for you to follow.

Remember to ask an adult to help you.

Cheddar Cheese Dog Cookies

You will need:

227g grated Cheddar cheese

(use at room temperature)

114g margarine

1 egg

1 clove of garlic (crushed)

172g wholewheat flour

30g wheatgerm

1 teaspoon salt

30ml milk

Preheat the oven to 375°F/190°C/gas mark 5.

Cream the cheese and margarine together.

When smooth, add the egg and garlic and mix well. Add the flour, wheatgerm and salt. Mix well until a dough forms. Add the milk and mix again.

Chill the mixture in the fridge for one hour.

Roll the dough onto a floured surface until it is about 4cm thick. Use cookie cutters to cut out shapes.

Bake on an ungreased baking tray for 15–18 minutes.

Cool to room temperature and store in an airtight container in the fridge.

There are lots of fun things on the website, including an online quiz, e-cards, colouring sheets and recipes for making dog and cat treats.

www.battersea.org.uk